P9-DFT-110

Dear Parents,

Welcome to the Scholastic Reader series. We have taken over 80 years of experience with teachers, parents, and children and put it into a program that is designed to match your child's interests and skills.

Level 1—Short sentences and stories made up of words kids can sound out using their phonics skills and words that are important to remember.

Level 2—Longer sentences and stories with words kids need to know and new "big" words that they will want to know.

Level 3—From sentences to paragraphs to longer stories, these books have large "chunks" of text and are made up of a rich vocabulary.

Level 4—First chapter books with more words and fewer pictures.

It is important that children learn to read well enough to succeed in school and beyond. Here are ideas for reading this book with your child:

- Look at the book together. Encourage your child to read the title and make a prediction about the story.
- Read the book together. Encourage your child to sound out words when appropriate. When your child struggles, you can help by providing the word.
- Encourage your child to retell the story. This is a great way to check for comprehension.
- Have your child take the fluency test on the last page to check progress.

Scholastic Readers are designed to support your child's efforts to learn how to read at every age and every stage. Enjoy helping your child learn to read and love to read.

—**Francie Alexander**
Chief Education Officer
Scholastic Education

Ms. Frizzle

Liz

Written by Joanna Cole.

Based on *The Magic School Bus* books written by Joanna Cole and illustrated by Bruce Degen.

The author and editor would like to thank Dr. Joni Johnson of the Astronomy Department of New Mexico State University for her advice in preparing this manuscript.

Illustrations by Carolyn Bracken.

No part of this publication may be reproduced in whole or in part, or stored in a retrieval system, or transmitted in any form or by any means, electronic, mechanical, photocopying, recording, or otherwise, without written permission of the publisher. For information regarding permission, write to Scholastic Inc., Attention: Permissions Department, 557 Broadway, New York, NY 10012.

ISBN 978-0-439-68400-2

Copyright © 2004 Joanna Cole and Bruce Degen. Published by Scholastic Inc. All rights reserved. SCHOLASTIC, THE MAGIC SCHOOL BUS, CARTWHEEL, and associated logos are trademarks and/or registered trademarks of Scholastic Inc.

26 25 24   40   14 15/0

Designed by Louise Bova & Maria Stasavage

Printed in the U.S.A.
First printing, September 2004

The Magic School Bus®

TAKES A MOONWALK

Arnold   Ralphie   Keesha   Phoebe   Carlos   Tim   Wanda   Dorothy Ann

Cartwheel
·B·O·O·K·S·®

SCHOLASTIC INC.

New York Toronto London Auckland
Sydney Mexico City New Delhi Hong Kong

Ms. Frizzle is not like most teachers.

We all get back on the bus.
Ms. Frizzle turns the key.
She pushes a bright button.

Now the bus goes above the clouds.
It goes to outer space.
We can see Earth behind us.
We can see the moon in front of us.

HOW WILL PHOEBE EXPLAIN
THIS TO HER DAD?

We wonder what Phoebe's dad will think.
We all look at Mr. Cox.
He doesn't know what to think.

We throw a rope to Mr. Cox.
It is a very long rope.
"Pull," Phoebe yells to us.

We get on the rocket ship.
Now it is time to go
back to Earth.
"Blast off," yells Ms. Frizzle.

When we reach the land,
the bus becomes a wagon.

We all sing on the hayride.
The moon is bright in the sky.

SHINING ON
by Phoebe

The harvest moon comes in the fall. At that time, the moon rises earlier in the evening, so it shines longer. It gives farmers more light to harvest their fields.

We are almost back to school.
The bus is back to being a bus again.

Our parents are waiting for us.
We are happy to be home for now.
Who knows what will happen tomorrow!

MORE ON THE MOON

◗ Earth is four times bigger than the moon.

◗ It takes about one month for the moon to go around Earth.
It takes Earth one year to go around the sun.

◗ The temperature on the moon can be as low as -247˚F (-155˚C)
in the dark. It can be as high as 221˚F (105˚C) in the sun.

MAN ON THE MOON

Neil Armstrong's moonwalk was on July 21, 1969.
Other astronauts have also walked on the moon.
Because there is no wind or weather on the moon, the astronauts'
footprints are still there. They will last for hundreds of years.

WHY DIDN'T THE COW JUMP OVER THE SUN?

ANSWER: SHE PREFERRED THE MOO-N!